# Purple Buttons

## ANGELA BULL

## Illustrated by Sue Porter

Oxford University Press

Oxford University Press, Great Clarendon Street, Oxford OX2 6DP

*Oxford New York*
*Athens Auckland Bangkok Bogota Bombay*
*Buenos Aires Calcutta Cape Town Dar es Salaam*
*Delhi Florence Hong Kong Istanbul Karachi*
*Kuala Lumpur Madras Madrid Melbourne*
*Mexico City Nairobi Paris Singapore*
*Taipei Tokyo Toronto*

and associated companies in
*Berlin Ibadan*

*Oxford* is a trade mark of Oxford University Press

Printed in Hong Kong

Illustrations by Sue Porter c/o Eunice McMullen Children's
Literary Agent Ltd.

Photo of Angela Bull by courtesy of the Craven Herald

Buttons! There's nothing special about
buttons! Rachel never knew there was,
until –

Until she saw Gran's buttons.

Rachel ran into Gran's house one day.
She had some good news.

'Our class at school is doing a play,' she said. 'I'm going to be the Queen.'

Gran looked pleased.

'What will you wear?' she asked.

'A long dress,' said Rachel, 'and a crown. Our teacher says I can make the crown myself, with gold paper. I can stick fruit gums on for jewels.'

'That sounds silly,' said Gran. 'Queens don't have sweets on their heads.'

Rachel thought for a minute.

'You're right,' she said. 'But – what could I use instead?'

'How about buttons?' said Gran.

Buttons!

'They might be good,' said Rachel. 'But I haven't got any.'

'I've got lots,' Gran told her. 'Fetch me the blue tin from the corner cupboard. I'll show you.'

Rachel carried the blue tin to Gran's table. Gran took off the lid, and tipped up the tin.

Out came a shower of buttons. Rachel
had never seen so many! They rattled and
spun and danced over the table. Rachel
had to catch two handfuls before they
rolled on to the floor.

Some were like tiny white daisies. Some
were like big splodgy snowflakes. There
were neat blackcurrants. There were bright
red cherries. There were pale lilac petals.

And they were all buttons!

'They're lovely!' cried Rachel. She
stopped. 'Most of them,' she said.

She'd seen the purple buttons.

She knew at once that she hated them.

The purple buttons were thin and slippery.

They were dark as bruises. They peeked up
at Rachel like sly, winking eyes.

'Why have you got these nasty purple
buttons, Gran?' Rachel asked.

'I keep all my buttons,' said Gran. 'I cut them off clothes that I've finished with. There's a story to every button.'

'Well, I don't like the purple ones,' said Rachel.

She pushed them away.

'I want some for jewels,' she said. 'To stick on my crown.'

She began to pick up the brightest,
shiniest buttons on the table. Some
sparkled like gold. Some gleamed like
silver. Some were warm scarlet. Some were
cool emerald.

'Can I borrow these?' she asked. 'Thank
you, Gran. You *are* kind!'

When she got home, she made her gold paper crown. She stuck Gran's buttons along the front. They were just like real jewels.

Everybody admired Rachel's crown.

When the play was over, Rachel took the buttons carefully off the crown. She was thinking. It would soon be her little brother Matthew's birthday.

'Gran,' she said, when she took the
buttons back. 'Can I borrow some more,
please? I want to stick them on the frill
round Matthew's birthday cake.'

Once more Gran tipped out her buttons.

'Orange and yellow, I think,' said
Rachel.

She scooped up a handful to choose
from – and dropped them.

Under the bright colours lurked the
purple buttons. They were so ugly! They
winked at Rachel with evil, goblin eyes.

'Where did you get these horrid buttons,
Gran?' she cried.

'They aren't horrid,' said Gran.

She took a purple button, and looked at
it closely.

'I cut them off a dress,' she said. 'I had it
when your Grandad was alive. It was a
nice dress, but things seemed to go wrong
when I wore it.'

'Like what?' asked Rachel.

'Once I broke my ankle,' said Gran. 'Once the car crashed. So I didn't want to wear the dress again. But I snipped off the buttons, and kept them.'

'What for?' said Rachel. She knew *she* would have thrown the nasty purple buttons away.

'You never know. They might come in handy one day,' said Gran.

She smiled, as if she liked the dark purple buttons.

Rachel chose nice bright ones for Matthew's birthday cake.

Not long afterwards, Rachel's Mum began to knit a cardigan for her. It was made of warm lilac wool, and it needed four buttons.

'Maybe Gran would lend you some buttons for it,' said Mum.

Rachel thought about Gran's buttons. She remembered the ones that looked like pale lilac petals. They would be perfect.

She asked about them, next time she went to see Gran.

'Is it all right if I borrow your lilac buttons for my new cardigan?' she said.

She fetched the blue tin from the
cupboard, and tipped the buttons onto the
table. She counted the lilac petals. Yes,
there were four! Just right.

'Can I take them home?' she asked.

Gran didn't answer.

Rachel looked at her. Gran was sitting in
her chair, with a very sad face.

'Gran!' cried Rachel. 'What's the matter?'

Gran held out her hand.

'It's my ring,' she said. 'I've lost one of the garnets out of it.'

'What are garnets?' Rachel asked.

'Those dark red stones. Can you see that one's missing?'

Rachel stared. There was a gap in the row of jewels on the ring.

'It must have fallen out,' said Gran sadly. 'I've hunted high and low, but I can't find it. And the ring's very special. Grandad gave it to me, forty years ago.'

3

Rachel jumped up. Gran had done a lot for her. She wanted to do something back.

'I'll look for it!' she said. 'It can't be far away.'

Gran shook her head.

'Don't bother,' she said. 'We'll never find it now. It's so tiny. Maybe it got swept up in the hoover.'

Rachel sat down again. She stared at the
buttons she'd tipped out. Some of Gran's
sadness seemed to have rubbed off on to
them. The white ones looked dull and
wishy-washy. The gold ones didn't shine
any longer. Even the lilac petals were
faded and dim.

Only the purple buttons still glittered on the table. They were thin and strange.

Wicked.

When Gran wore them on a dress, bad things happened. Now, bad things were happening again.

It must be their fault.

'I *hate* the purple buttons!' Rachel cried.

She flicked one as hard as she could. It spun across the room, into a far corner.

'Hey!' exclaimed Gran. 'Stop it! I like my buttons. I don't want to lose them as well as the garnet.'

She looked quite cross. Rachel felt awful. 'Sorry, Gran,' she said.

She flew to the corner where the button had fallen. She ran her hands along the carpet, trying to find it.

Something winked. Something glinted.
Rachel peered down. There was the purple
button! But it wasn't lying flat. It slanted,
as if it was half propped up.

What could it be propped against?

Rachel lifted it with the tip of her finger.
Hidden under the button lay a tiny red
jewel.

Rachel's heart thumped, as if she'd run from one end of the playground to the other. She picked up the jewel and the button, and held them out.

'Gran! Look!' she said.

'Oh!' cried Gran. 'The garnet from my
ring.'

Her face was so happy again.

'I found it under the purple button,' said
Rachel.

She was smiling too.

'Then it's lucky you flicked the button off the table,' said Gran. 'The nice, purple button.'

'Why do you like it so much, Gran?' Rachel asked.

'Because it's pretty,' said Gran. 'You might think so too, if you looked at it properly.'

For the first time, Rachel looked at the button as hard as she could. Her eyes opened wide with surprise.

'Yes!' she said. 'It's lovely!'

The button shone with a pale, pearly glow. Its rim was carved like a shell. And it wasn't thin and slippery. It was slim, and smooth, and elegant.

Quickly, Rachel picked up the other purple buttons from the table. She counted them. One, two, three, four. Just right!

'Gran,' she said. 'You know I need four buttons for my new cardigan. Could I borrow the purple ones?'

'Of course,' said Gran. 'Don't forget, I told you they might come in handy one day.'

# About the author

When I was a little girl, my mother kept buttons
in a shiny, six-sided tin. As a treat, she sometimes
let me play with them, sort them out and make
them into patterns. So I wrote
a story about another girl,
Rachel, who enjoys buttons.

When my own two
children were small, I kept
my buttons in a jamjar. Not
so interesting! Now that
I've got two grandchildren
as well, I must find a
proper, shiny button tin.

I live in the country, and I've written lots
of children's books.